Michael Dahl

Yap Kun Rong

Rain

Raintree is an imprint of Capstone Global Library
Limited, a company incorporated in England and Wales
having its registered office at 7 Pilgrim Street, London,
EC4V 6LB – Registered company number: 6695582

"Raintree" is a registered trademark
of Pearson Education Limited, under licence
to Capstone Global Library Limited

Text © Stone Arch Books 2009
First published in the United Kingdom in hardback
and paperback by Capstone Global Library in 2010
The moral rights of the proprietor have been asserted.

Creative Director: Heather Kindseth
Graphic Designer: Brann Garvey
UK Editor: Vaarunika Dharmapala
Originated by Capstone Global Library Ltd
Printed and bound in China by South China
Printing Company Ltd

ISBN 978 1 406215 17 5 (hardback)
14 13 12 11 10
10 9 8 7 6 5 4 3 2 1

ISBN 978 1 406215 31 1 (paperback)
14 13 12 11 10
10 9 8 7 6 5 4 3 2 1

British Library Cataloguing in Publication Data
A full catalogue record for this book is available from
the British Library.

CONTENTS

Introduction

A new Age of Dragons is about to begin. The powerful creatures will return to rule the world once more, but this time it will be different. This time, they will have allies who will help them. Around the world, some young humans are making a strange discovery. They are learning that they were born with dragon blood – blood that gives them amazing powers.

CHAPTER 1
Strange Blood

A van stopped near a lonely farmhouse in northern Canada.

The van was a **bloodmobile**.

During the day, the driver drove to schools and hospitals so that people could donate blood.

This afternoon, the driver shut off the van's engine and checked her records.

A boy named Sam Stevens had donated blood at a school last week.

But there was something strange about the donation.

Sam Stevens had lizard blood in his veins.

"There must be a mistake," the driver said to herself.

The driver wanted to talk to Sam Stevens.

She believed the boy needed to see a doctor.

The driver walked up to the
front door of Sam's house.

The *windows* of the house were
dark.

When she knocked, there was
no answer.

Then she saw a *light* moving
through the forest.

CHAPTER 2
THE TOWER

Someone was walking among the trees next to the farmhouse.

Quietly, the driver walked into the woods.

As she got closer to the *light*, the driver saw a man.

The man was carrying food
on a tray.

He also held a lantern and
a rifle.

The man walked through the
trees towards a stone tower.

The driver followed him.

A clanking sound came from
inside the tower.

CHAPTER 3
IN CHAINS

The driver peeked around the door.

The man placed the tray of food on the floor.

A boy sat in front of the man.

The boy was **chained** to the wall of the tower.

"Who came up the driveway?" asked the boy.

"Never mind," said the man. "Eat your dinner, Sam."

Suddenly, Sam began to **shake**. The chains **rattled**.

"I can't stay here forever," he cried.

"It's for your own protection,"
said the man.

Sam looked down at the strange **birthmark** on his arm.

"I'm different," he said. "I can't change that. It's in my **blood**."

Then Sam added *quietly*, "They're coming for me. I know they are."

CHAPTER 4
DRAGON CRY

Something **roared** in the forest.

Sam began to sweat.

As the driver watched, wings sprouted from the boy's back.

Sharp claws grew out of his fingers.

Sam's face became long and pointed.

Another roar **shook** the forest.

"I'll never let them take you away," said the man.

He grabbed his rifle.

The driver, standing at the door, turned around.

Behind her stood a scaly creature with wings.

It was a dragon.

The driver ran inside the tower as the dragon lunged forward.

Its huge jaws pushed against the doorway.

The man used his rifle to attack the creature.

The dragon was not scared off.

The small dragon that used to be Sam pulled against the chains.

Both creatures roared at each other.

All night the **large dragon** tried to enter the tower.

The driver and the man worked together to fight the creature.

Then a mighty wind shook the forest.

Trees groaned and creaked.

The huge dragon turned and flew off into the night sky.

Sam returned to his normal shape.

He lay, tired and sweating, on the floor of the tower.

"I told you I wouldn't let them get you, Sam," said the man.

Sam smiled weakly.

"It'll be back," said Sam.

"And I'll be waiting for it," said
the man.

He turned to the driver and said,
"Lucky for us you were here."

z z z Z

When Sam fell asleep, the
driver stepped outside.

Morning *light* began to fill the
peaceful forest.

Will it be peaceful tomorrow night?
she wondered.

Of Dragons and Near-Dragons

If dragons lived on Earth, they would probably communicate with each other the way other reptiles do.

Many reptiles hiss by blowing air through their mouths.

Snakes can hear a human speaking from 3 metres (10 feet) away. Some scientists believe that snakes can also feel vibrations from other snakes many kilometres away.

The tuatara lizard of New Zealand has no outside ears. But it can still hear!

Some lizards communicate by doing push-ups! They bob up and down to warn other lizards to stay away from their territory.

Baby alligators chirp inside their eggs. They tell their mothers it is time to dig up the eggs from the dirt. They are ready to hatch!

ABOUT THE AUTHOR

Michael Dahl is the author of more than 200 books for children and young adults. He has won the AEP Distinguished Achievement Award three times for his non-fiction. His *Finnegan Zwake* mystery series was shortlisted twice by the Anthony and Agatha awards. He has also written the *Library of Doom* series. He is a featured speaker at conferences around the country on graphic novels and high-interest books for boys.

ABOUT THE ILLUSTRATOR

Yap Kun Rong is a freelance illustrator and concept artist for books, comics, and video games.

GLOSSARY

allies people or countries that give support to each other

birthmark mark on the skin that was there from birth

creaked made a squeaky, grating noise

creature living thing that is human or animal

donate give something freely. A donation is a gift that is given without getting a reward.

lunged moved forward quickly and suddenly

rule have power over something

sprouted grew, appeared, or developed quickly

DISCUSSION QUESTIONS

1. Do you think it was safe for the driver to go to the farmhouse? Why or why not?

2. What or who did you think was locked in the tower? Explain your answer.

3. If you were the author, what would you have named this book? Why?

WRITING PROMPTS

1. The author gives a couple of clues that Sam is a dragon. Find the clues and make a list.

2. Why do you think the other dragon was trying to get Sam? Write a paragraph explaining your reasons.

3. What do you think would have happened to Sam and the man if the driver hadn't been there? Rewrite the ending without the driver.

MORE BOOKS TO READ

LIBRARY OF DOOM

Meet the mysterious Librarian. Keeper of the world's most dangerous books, sworn enemy of monsters made of paper and ink, crusader of young people threatened by ancient curses... Enter the Library of Doom to follow these heart-pounding adventures.